Scarecrow

WRITTEN BY

Cynthia Rylant

ILLUSTRATED BY

Lauren Stringer

Voyager Books
Harcourt, Inc.
Orlando Austin New York
San Diego Toronto London

His hat is borrowed, his suit is borrowed, his hands are borrowed, even his head is borrowed. And his eyes probably came out of someone's drawer.

But a scarecrow's life is all his own.

It takes a certain peace, hanging around a garden all day. It takes a love of silence and air. A liking for long, slow thoughts. A friendliness toward birds.

Yes, birds. Crows, grackles, starlings, jays. Ask them how they feel about a scarecrow, and they'll say, "Lovely." They ignore the pie-pan hands and the button eyes and see instead the scarecrow's best gift: his gentleness.

They line up on his arms
and can chat all day.

He knows he isn't real. A scarecrow understands right away that he is just borrowed parts made to look like somebody.

But he knows this, too: that there is a certain wonder going on around him. Seeds are being planted, and inside them there are ten-foot-tall sunflowers and mammoth pumpkins and beans that just go on forever.

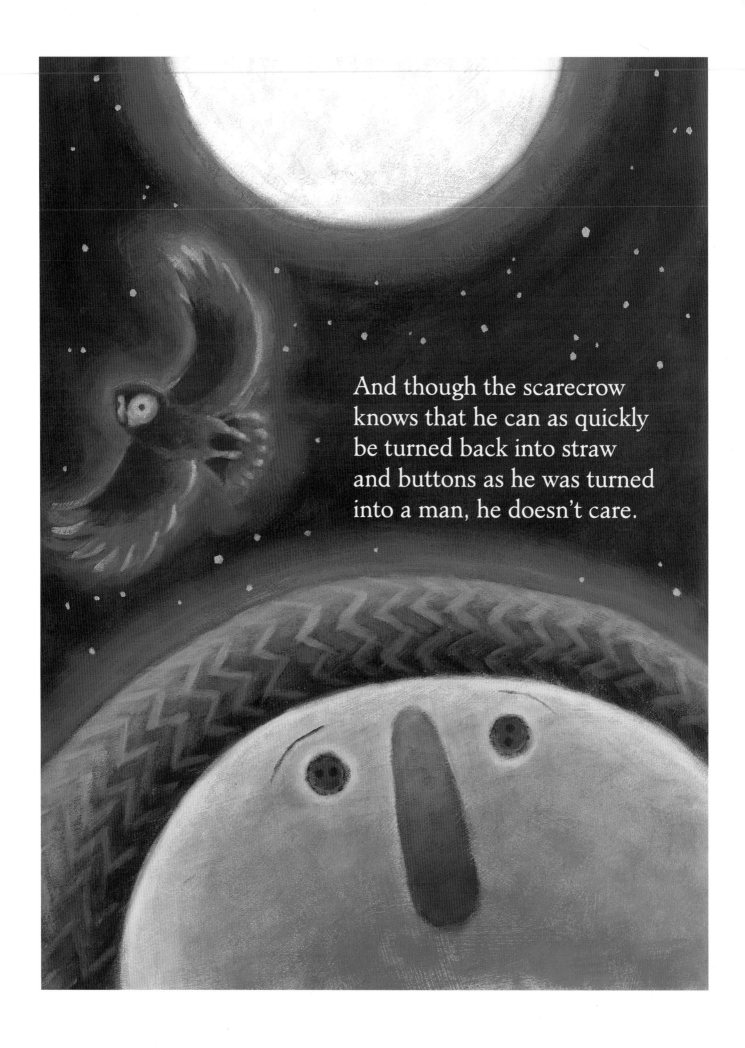

And though the scarecrow
knows that he can as quickly
be turned back into straw
and buttons as he was turned
into a man, he doesn't care.

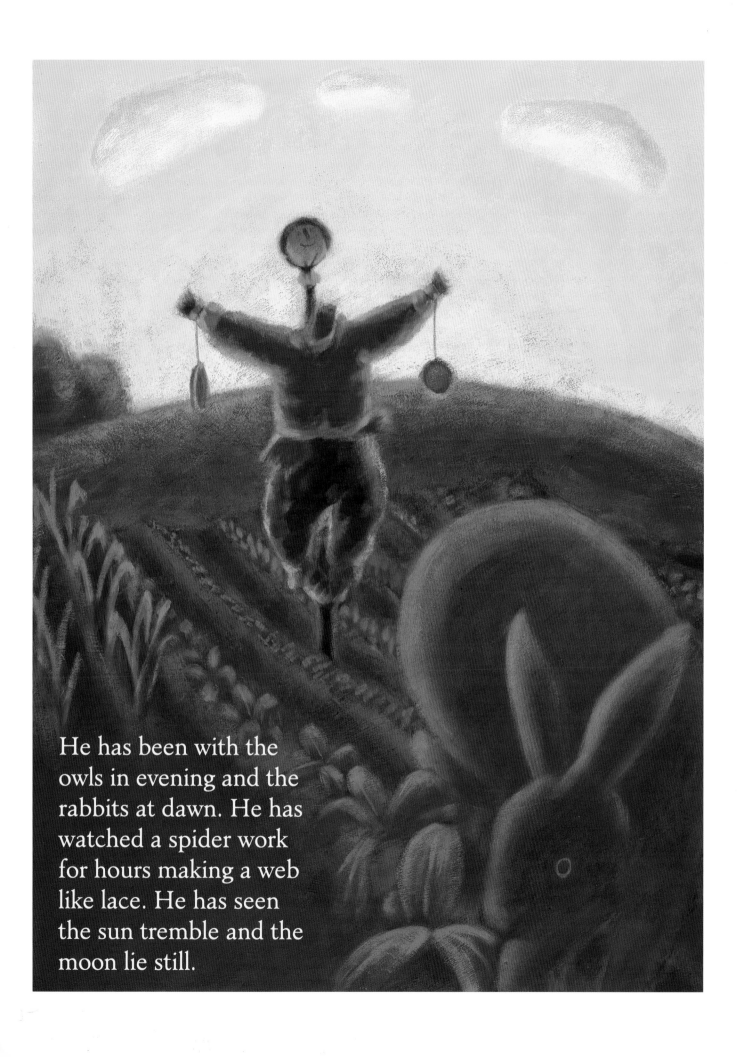

He has been with the owls in evening and the rabbits at dawn. He has watched a spider work for hours making a web like lace. He has seen the sun tremble and the moon lie still.

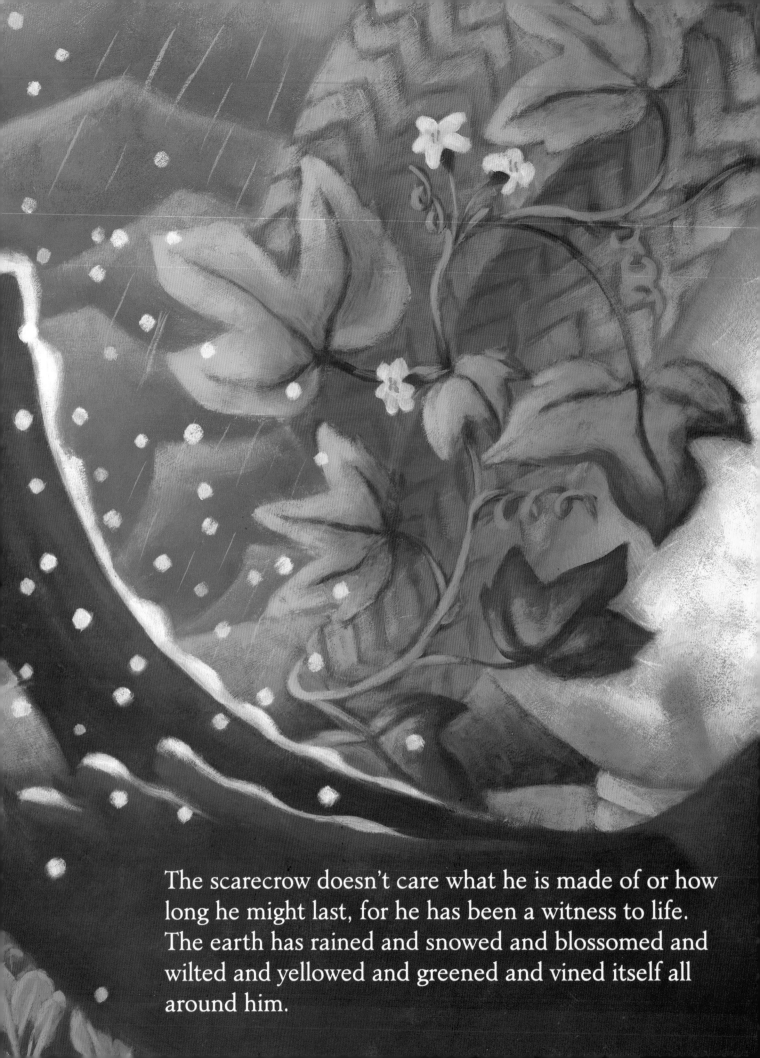

The scarecrow doesn't care what he is made of or how long he might last, for he has been a witness to life. The earth has rained and snowed and blossomed and wilted and yellowed and greened and vined itself all around him.

His hat has housed mice and
his arms have rested birds.
A morning glory has held tight
to his legs and a worm is living
in his lapel.

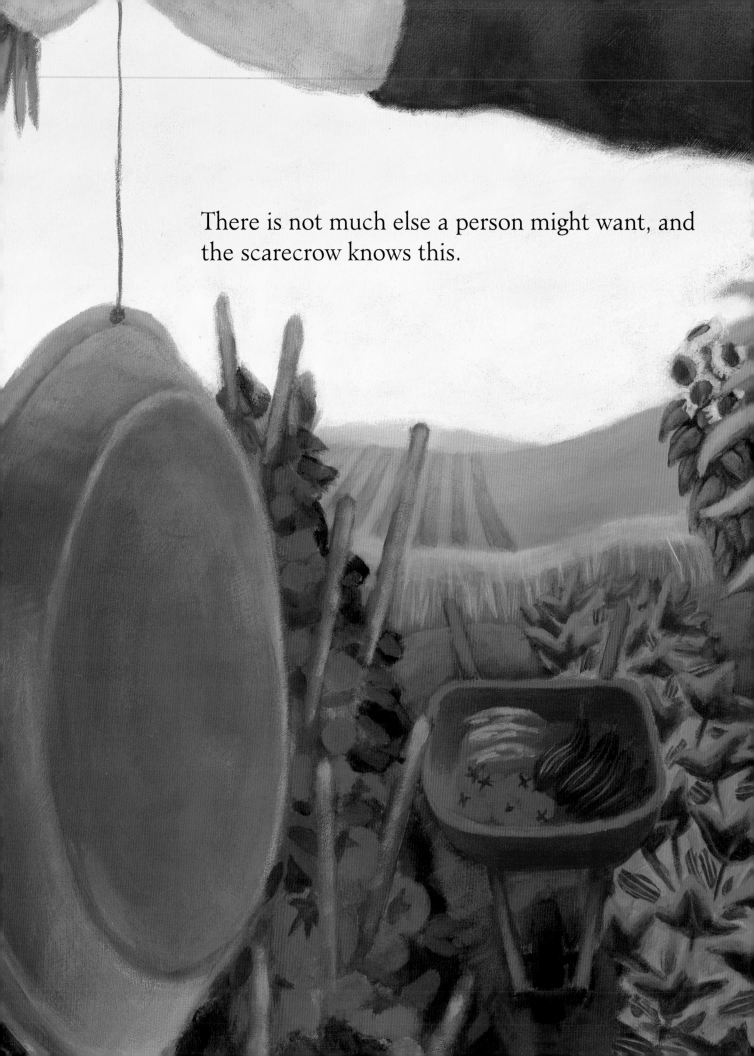

There is not much else a person might want, and the scarecrow knows this.

So he doesn't mind that there is always a smile on his face or that his eyes are always open. He doesn't mind being up high. He doesn't mind staying there.

The wind is brushing his borrowed head
and the sun is warming his borrowed hands
and clouds are floating across his
button-borrowed eyes.

The scarecrow is thinking his long, slow thoughts . . .

. . . and soon, birds will
be coming by.

For Rubin Pfeffer,
who inspired this
—C. R.

For Matthew,
who fills my life with colors
I can see and hear
—L. S.

Requests for permission to make copies of any part of the work should be
submitted online at www.harcourt.com/contact or mailed to the following address:
Permissions Department, Harcourt, Inc., 6277 Sea Harbor Drive, Orlando, Florida 32887-6777.

www.HarcourtBooks.com

First Voyager Books edition 2001
Voyager Books is a trademark of Harcourt, Inc.,
registered in the United States of America and other jurisdictions.

The Library of Congress has cataloged the hardcover edition as follows:
Rylant, Cynthia.
Scarecrow/Cynthia Rylant; illustrated by Lauren Stringer.
p. cm.
Summary: Although made of straw and borrowed clothes,
a scarecrow appreciates his peaceful, gentle life
and the privilege of watching nature at work.
[1. Scarecrows—Fiction.] I. Stringer, Lauren, ill. II. Title.
PZ7.R982Sc 1998
[E]—dc20 96-7652
ISBN-13: 978-0-15-201084-3 ISBN-10: 0-15-201084-X
ISBN-13: 978-0-15-202480-2 pb ISBN-10: 0-15-202480-8 pb

M O Q R P N L

The illustrations in this book were done in Lascaux acrylics on
Arches 150-lb. watercolor paper.
The display type was set in OptiMarcus.
The text type was set in Minister Light.
Color separations by Bright Arts, Ltd., Singapore
Printed and bound by Tien Wah Press, Singapore
Production supervision by Sandra Grebenar and Pascha Gerlinger
Designed by Lauren Stringer and Lydia D'moch